TELEPEN

D1323783

EL

e Butel

WITHDRAWN

LIBRARY

CHRIST CHURCH COLLEGE CANTERBURY

This book must be returned (or renewed)
or before the date last marked.

Items required f   R
Term Loan

Methuen Children's Books

Once upon a time
there was a little pink pig . . .

who had a smart red umbrella!

One day he put on his new white gloves and went out for a walk.

The sky was bright blue. Even so,
the little pink pig wanted to take
his smart red umbrella with him.

On the way he stopped. He sat down
at the edge of a grassy green field,

and began to pick some pretty yellow
buttercups.

Suddenly big black clouds filled the sky.

The little pink pig got up quickly
and hurried off.

Oh! A big drop of grey rain fell on
the end of his pink nose!

The little pig began to laugh.
'*I'm* not afraid of the rain.
I've got my smart umbrell . . . oh!'

'Oh dear!' exclaimed the little pig.
'I've left my umbrella
in the grassy green field!'

He began to run as fast as he could
back to the grassy green field, but
the rain fell harder and harder.
It rained so hard . . .

that the little pig was wet through
by the time he found his umbrella.

He picked it up and opened it.

All at once the sun began to shine again.
The little pig danced in the sun,
and soon he was dry again.